Why Don't I Fit In?

Sharon Meyerhoff Pezan

Illustrated by Teri Runte-Peacock

ISBN 978-1-0980-7478-4 (paperback)
ISBN 978-1-0980-9559-8 (hardcover)
ISBN 978-1-0980-7479-1 (digital)

Christian Faith Publishing, Inc.
832 Park Avenue
Meadville, PA 16335
www.christianfaithpublishing.com

Printed in the United States of America

To my grandson, Christian Gabrial,
who inspires me with his creativity

Have you ever felt like you didn't fit in?

Once upon a time, there was an older gentleman whose name was Charlie. He owned a beautiful red car that he called Big Red.

Charlie kept Big Red shiny. He loved to clean and wax his car. Big Red had a wonderful life. His owner loved him and was proud to drive him around the neighborhood.

Charlie drove Big Red to church each Sunday; everyone at church thought of Big Red as family.

One day Charlie did not come out to see Big Red.
He didn't come out to drive his red car, wash it,
or wax it. Charlie never came out anymore.

One day, Red saw an ambulance pull into the driveway, and then Big Red was left alone.

A few weeks later, Charlie's son came to the house and put up a for sale sign, and drove Big Red across the road into an old shed.

But Big Red didn't fit. Only the front end of the
beautiful car fit in. No one came to see him, to
drive him, to wash him, or wax him.
He missed Charlie.

He didn't understand why he didn't fit in. Was he too big, the wrong color, too tall, or too short? He didn't realize the old broken-down shed was not a garage; it wasn't built to be a home for a car.

Actually, when Red thought about
the shed, he felt sorry for the shed
with all its broken pieces.

In fact, it was hard for anyone to
see the once-beautiful red car.

Other cars passing by honked at him,
some made fun of him, some laughed
at the red car that didn't fit in.

It made Big Red feel blue. He
didn't know what to do.

He was out in all the weather; the rain fell hard
and there was no one to put on the windshield
wipers. There was no one to brush off the falling
snow. There was no one to keep up the tires. He
started to rust, his lights were never on, and he
felt alone in the darkness and became sad.

Other cars passed by. Some still
laughed at the car who didn't fit in.
The grass grew up around him and
no one seemed to notice or care.

Until one day, Charlie's son came
to see him with a family, a mom,
dad, and two little children.

Red loved kids. He brightened up.

They put the familiar key in and turned
the car on, and the car was so happy. He
sparkled with delight; someone wanted
him. The family got in and carefully backed
him out of the falling down shed; they were
smiling, they were happy. They had been
looking for just the right car for their family.

They fell in love with Big Red. They drove him home where they had a big garage for Red. They drove him right in, and he fit.

They cleaned and waxed the car until it shined. They sang as the whole family helped to fix all the rust spots and Big Red was smiling tire to tire.

He was so happy. You see, God has a plan for each of us before we ever set out on the road. Sometimes it feels as if we don't fit in where we are, but in God's plan, we all eventually fit in.

About the Author

As of this writing, Sharon lives with her husband, Ralph, and her seventeen animals outside Apple River, Illinois. Sharon's animals include four beautiful and extremely friendly horses, one miniature donkey that counts out her age, seven dogs, and five cats. Sharon has one daughter, happily married with our first grandson. Sharon has many animal stories that she hopes to write about in the future.

To
Evangeline
I hope you enjoy the
Story of Big Red –
Be Happy Be Safe,
Be Joyful in Life
God Bless You
♡

Sharon

July 2021

CPSIA information can be obtained
at www.ICGtesting.com
Printed in the USA
JSHW010046150621
15910JS00003B/13